THE WATCHING GAME

THE WATCHING GAME

by Louise Borden

Illustrated by Teri Weidner

SCHOLASTIC INC.
New York   Toronto   London   Auckland   Sydney

ISBN 0-590-43595-7

Text copyright © 1991 by Louise Borden.
Illustrations copyright © 1991 by Teri Weidner.
All rights reserved. Published by Scholastic Inc.

12 11 10 9 8 7 6 5 4 3 2 1   10   2 3 4 5 6 7 8/9

Printed in the U.S.A.   08

For my mother and Dots,
who know about minnow nets;
and for Grace Mac,
who knows about words
—LB

For my mother and father
—TW

Nana lives in the country,
where the trees stand cold in winter
and fields are brown in the sun.
In her barn hang some sleds
for cousins,
for me.

When the snow gusts white across her fields,
we come to stay in her big gray house.
All of us...Gordon and Blair, Jess and me.

And Nana's fox lives down
by the edge of her woods,
just where our sleds stop
and the beech trees begin.
Sometimes we call him Lickety-Quick,
and sometimes we just call him Nana's fox.

We play a watching game, all the cousins.
And when we see him,
Nana says we'll put out Grandpa's hat,
the one that he wore fishing
all those years ago.
"Then," Nana says,
"that fox will know when he's been seen."

I wonder when we're watching
if the fox is watching for us.
I wonder when I'm watching
if the fox is watching for me.

Blair sees him first,
all bushy, rusty tail
waving behind him like a flag.
Then Nana sees him again
just when the sun is going down.

I know someday I'll see him first,
that flash of a fox,
and I'll feel Grandpa's smooth old hat,
soft as a quilt in my hands.

Nana lives in the country,
where in the spring,
clouds billow fat in the sky
and stars fill wide, dark nights.
On her tree hang some swings
for cousins,
for me.

When the warm rains beat upon Nana's roof,
I lie on the long gray boards of her kitchen floor
with paths for marbles, roads for cars.
I've counted them, seventeen to the stove.
Gordon, who's sleepy, sits by the window,
watching through the rain for Nana's fox.
He wants to be the next one to put out Grandpa's hat.
But I think old Lickety-Quick is dry inside a mossy log.

In summer, we come again to Nana's,
where the night crickets chirr us to sleep
and lightning bugs gleam in jars.
On her pond are some rowboats
for cousins,
for me.

When the sun glimmers hot on the water,
we stop our fishing to play the watching game.
Our minnow nets drip puddles in the bottom of the boats.

"There! Did you see him?"
Blair, who never keeps her minnows,
points across the fields.
But old Lickety-Quick is faster than minnows.

"Must have been a shadow..." the rest of us say,
dipping our nets back into the water.
So Grandpa's hat stays hanging on the hook
in our grandmother's hall.

We come in from the sun,

leaving buckets of minnows
in a row outside.

On Nana's wall we play with shadows.
Blair makes one that looks like Nana's fox.

"He's asleep in the shade today."
That's what Nana says.
But we watch for him,
crossing our fingers
all the same.

Nana lives in the country
where autumn leaves turn gold
beyond her windows.
I wonder if her fox knows
that we've come again.
On her porch are some pumpkins
for cousins,
for me.

I ask Nana to put out another one,
right next to mine,
for Lickety-Quick.
Jess says foxes don't care about pumpkins.
But I paint a sign anyway
to let him know that it's from me.

FOR LICKETY
Quick from
Gray

And old Lickety-Quick keeps out of sight
down by the edge of Nana's woods.
Nana says he listens for hounds
and watches across October fields
as the fox hunters ride on by.

Nana lives in the country,
not lonely, just alone.
With boats and stars and rustling trees,
with swings and fields and a fox running free.

And today he sees me watching.
Today he is watching for me.